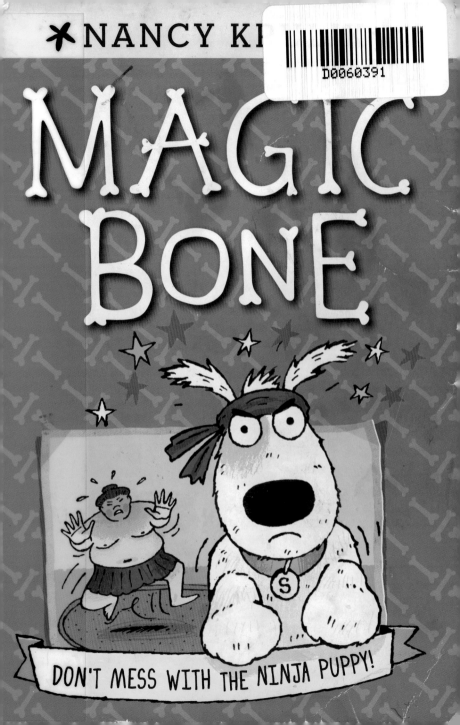

NANCY KR

D0060391

MAGIC
BONE

DON'T MESS WITH THE NINJA PUPPY!

EAN

ISBN 978-0-448-48095-4

9 780448 480954

50499>

MAGIC BONE

DON'T MESS WITH THE NINJA PUPPY!

GROSSET & DUNLAP
Published by the Penguin Group
Penguin Group (USA) LLC, 375 Hudson Street, New York, New York 10014, USA

USA | Canada | UK | Ireland | Australia | New Zealand | India | South Africa | China

penguin.com
A Penguin Random House Company

If you purchased this book without a cover, you should be aware that this book is stolen property. It was reported as "unsold and destroyed" to the publisher, and neither the author nor the publisher has received any payment for this "stripped book."

Penguin supports copyright. Copyright fuels creativity, encourages diverse voices, promotes free speech, and creates a vibrant culture. Thank you for buying an authorized edition of this book and for complying with copyright laws by not reproducing, scanning, or distributing any part of it in any form without permission. You are supporting writers and allowing Penguin to continue to publish books for every reader.

The publisher does not have any control over and does not assume any responsibility for author or third-party websites or their content.

Text copyright © 2014 by Nancy Krulik. Illustrations copyright © 2014 by Sebastien Braun. All rights reserved. Published by Grosset & Dunlap, a division of Penguin Young Readers Group, 345 Hudson Street, New York, New York 10014. GROSSET & DUNLAP is a trademark of Penguin Group (USA) LLC. Printed in the USA.

Library of Congress Cataloging-in-Publication Data is available.

ISBN 978-0-448-48095-4   10 9 8 7 6 5 4 3 2

MAGIC BONE

DON'T MESS WITH THE NINJA PUPPY!

by Nancy Krulik
illustrated by Sebastien Braun

Grosset & Dunlap
An Imprint of Penguin Group (USA) LLC

For Amanda, who sees the
magic in everything!—NK

For Aidan—SB

CHAPTER 1

Clickety, clackety. Jingle, jangle.

My paws start bouncing. My tail starts wagging. I know what those sounds mean.

My Josh is home! He's at the door! I leap off the couch and run toward the door.

Whoops. My tail accidentally knocked something hard and clunky off the table.

Oops. My paws step right on that hard-and-clunky something.

Suddenly that big box against

the wall turns on. The tiny two-legs inside the box start talking to me. Where did they come from?

I can't think about that now. Josh is home. That's all I can think about.

I run over and start scratching at the door. "Hurry, Josh!" I bark to him.

The *clickety-clackety* things keep jingle jangling at the door.

I keep scratching.

Jingle, jangle.

Scratchity, scratch, scratch.

The door opens. And there he is! My Josh.

My tail wags harder. "Josh!" I bark happily. "Josh! Jo—"

Wait a minute. Who's that with Josh? It's a girl two-leg. She's been here before. She and Josh like to play catch in our backyard. Sometimes they let me play. But not always.

"Are you going to play with me today?" I bark to the girl two-leg. "Are you?"

"Sparky, stop!" Josh yells at me.

I don't understand a lot of two-leg words. But I understand those two. So I stop barking.

Josh pets me on the head and

starts talking to the girl two-leg. It sounds like, "Sophie. Blah, blah, blah. Sophie. Blah, blah, blah. Sophie."

I think the two-leg must be called Sophie.

Sophie sits down on the couch. She smiles at Josh and says something that sounds like, "Josh, come."

Josh walks over to her.

Then, Sophie pats the couch and says, "Sit."

Josh sits beside her on the couch.

This is very strange. Usually Josh is the one who says things like *come* and *sit*. And I'm the one who comes and sits beside him. I do that because Josh is in charge of me. I wonder if Sophie is in charge of Josh?

Josh and Sophie sit on the couch

for a long, long time. They say a lot of two-leg things I do not understand. They watch the teeny, tiny two-legs who live inside the box.

Then Sophie stands up. She says some more two-leg words. The only word I understand is *go*. And Josh goes—right toward the door.

Wow. I guess Sophie *is* in charge.

I start to follow Josh and Sophie outside. But Josh says, "Sparky, stay."

I stop following. I know what *stay* means.

As Josh closes the door behind him, I jump up onto the couch and look out the window. I watch as Josh and Sophie get into the metal machine with the four round paws and go away.

Wiggle, waggle, boo. I'm alone with nothing to do.

Wait a minute! I know something I can do all by myself. Something really, really fun.

I squeeze my way through my doggie door and out into our backyard. I race over to Josh's flower bed. And I start to dig. *Diggety, dig, dig.* I'm a great digger.

Dirt flies everywhere. I'm digging a hole. A deep, deep hole. *Diggety, dig . . .*

Wow! Look at that!

It's a bone. A bright, beautiful, sparkly bone. Sitting right in the middle of my hole.

Sniffety, sniff, sniff. This bone smells good. Like chicken, beef, and sausage all rolled into one.

I just *have* to take a bite . . . *Chomp!*

Wiggle, waggle, whew. I feel dizzy—like my insides are spinning all around—but my outsides are standing still. Stars are twinkling in front of my eyes—even though it's daytime! All around me I smell food—fried chicken, salmon, roast beef. But there isn't any food in sight.

And then . . .

Kaboom! Kaboom! Kaboom!

CHAPTER 2

The *kabooming* stops.

I look around. I'm definitely not in my yard anymore. I can tell because there are lots of trees here. I only have one tree in my yard.

There are lots of two-legs here, too. There's only one two-leg in my yard—Josh. And maybe, sometimes, Sophie.

What's going on? How did I get here?

Wait a minute. I know. It was my bone. My *magic* bone. I chomped down on it, and *kaboom*! Here I am.

Wherever *here* is.

This isn't the first time my magic bone has *kaboomed* me somewhere. It's done it before. Like the time it took me all the way to London. Talk about a *yummy, yum, yum* place! You wouldn't believe all the sausage, fish, and chips the two-legs dropped on the ground! And every dog knows: If it's on the floor, it's dog food!

Another time, my magic bone *kaboomed* me to Rome! The meatballs in Rome were delicious! But the cats were really mean. Which didn't surprise me. I know a cat at home named Queenie who is the meanest thing on four paws.

Once I chomped into my bone and ended up in Switzerland. It snowed so hard there I could barely see. Luckily for me, my nose could still sniff, because it sniffed out some *yummy, yum, yum* cheese.

I sure hope they have some yummy food in this place. I can't wait to start exploring.

But first, I have to bury my bone. I don't want some other dog finding it. I'm going to need it again. My magic bone is the only way I can get back to Josh.

I carry my bone over to a big tree that is right across from a giant water bowl. There's water shooting up from the middle of the water bowl.

I'm going to bury my bone next to

this tree. That way, when it's time for me to dig up my bone and go home, all I will have to do is look for the tree that is right across from the water that sprays up into the sky.

I start digging. Dirt flies. The hole gets deeper and deeper.

I drop my bone into the hole and push the dirt right back over it. Now my bone is completely hidden. No one will ever find it—except me, of course!

All that digging was hard work. It's time to play. But is there anyone here for me to play with?

I see a group of two-legs over on the grass. They're smiling. And laughing. And dancing around.

I know how to dance. I learned when the magic bone *kaboomed* me to Hawaii. A two-leg named Lolani took me to her hula-dance school. Lolani made me wear grass around my belly when I danced. That was strange. But the dancing was fun.

"Me too! Me too!" I bark as I run

over to the group of dancing two-legs.

I stand on my hind legs, and I twirl around.

The two-legs laugh.

I keep twirling. Fast. Faster. *Fastest.* Twirl, twirl, twirl. *Wiggle, waggle, whoa* . . . I'm getting dizzy.

I stop twirling.

But everything around me keeps on twirling. And swirling. And whirling.

Splat. I fall down on my belly.

The two-legs laugh harder.

"That wasn't funny," I bark. "You're being mean."

Sniff, sniff, sniff.

Hey! There's someone sniffing my butt! *Sniff, sniff, sniff.*

"Are you okay?"

I turn around and come face-to-face . . . with a big Akita. Well, face-to-neck, really. The Akita is very tall.

"Yeah," I tell her. "I just was twirling too much."

The Akita stares at me for a minute. "You're not from around here, are you?"

I shake my head. "I'm from Josh's house," I say.

"Where's Josh's house?" she asks me.

"Next to Josh's yard," I tell her. "Whose yard is this?"

"This isn't a yard," the Akita says. "It's a park. Yoyogi Park."

"Yo . . . yo . . . gi," I say slowly. "That's a funny name."

The Akita bares her teeth and growls. "No, it's not. It's a beautiful name for a beautiful park."

Wiggle, waggle, uh-oh! I don't want

to make this Akita angry. She's got sharp teeth and a scary look in her eyes.

"It's a very beautiful park," I agree quickly. "Um . . . my name is Sparky. What's yours?"

The Akita smiles, a little. "I'm Nanami," she says. "*Kon'nichiwa,* Sparky."

"Kon'nich-*what*?" I ask.

"*Kon'nichiwa,*" she says again. "That's how we say *hello* here in Tokyo."

Tokyo! That must be the name of this place.

"*Kon'nichiwa,*" I slowly say back to Nanami.

Grumble. Rumble. Suddenly, my tummy starts talking. I speak

17

tummy. So I know "grumble, rumble," means "feed me!"

"Do two-legs share food with dogs in Tokyo?" I ask Nanami. "They do in some places. In Rome, some dogs get to sit right at the table with their two-legs."

"Rome?" Nanami asks. "Is that where Josh's house is?"

I shake my head. "No. I went to Rome because my mag—"

Whoops. I stop talking right away. I don't want to tell Nanami about my magic bone. That's my secret.

"Um . . . no," I say quickly. "I just was in Rome once."

"Oh," Nanami says. "Well, here some two-legs share. I know a place where you can get food. Do you want to go with me?"

My tail starts wagging. My paws get ready to run. *"Wiggle, waggle, woo-hoo!* I sure do!"

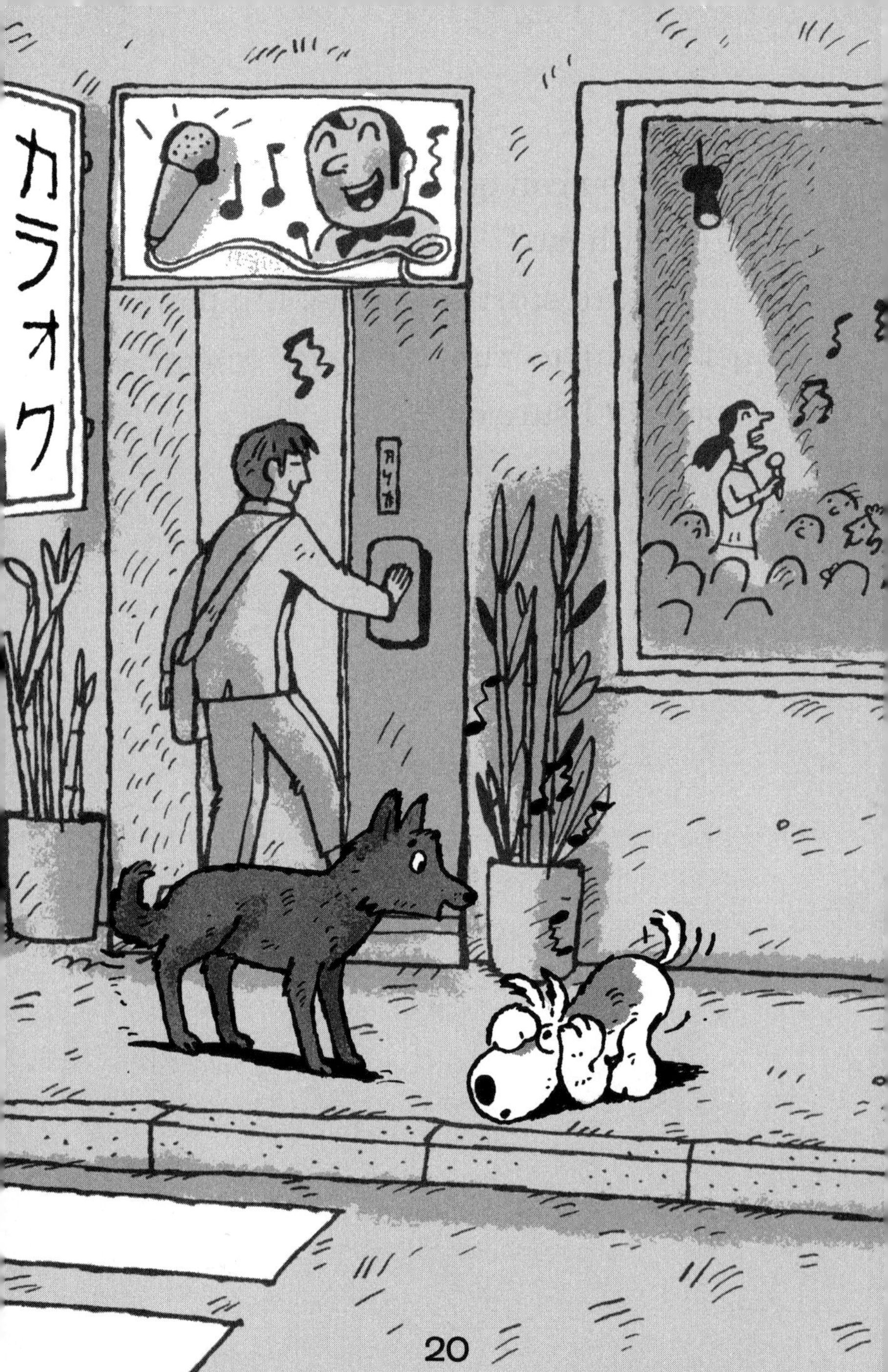
カラオク

CHAPTER 3

Owie, ow, ow!

Nanami and I haven't been running long when I hear a terrible noise. It's loud and screechy. And it hurts my ears.

I cover my ears with my paws. But I can still hear the noise. *Owie, ow, ow!*

"What's that?" I ask Nanami.

"A two-leg howling in the karaoke club." Nanami points to a building with open windows.

"Kara-*whatee* club?" I ask.

"Karaoke club," Nanami repeats. "It's a place where two-legs howl while music plays."

I don't know what *music* is, but I know howling when I hear it.

"See?" Nanami says. "There's a two-leg howling up there in the front."

I peek through one of the open doors. Sure enough, there's a two-leg standing up. She's squawking. And squeaking. It's awful.

And then, suddenly, the squeaking and squawking stops.

"Hooray!" I bark happily.

The two-legs inside begin to hit their paws together. It makes a funny sound. *Clap. Clap. Clap.*

I also try to hit my front paws

together, but they don't make any sounds.

Just then, a two-leg comes out of the karaoke club. *Uh-oh*. I know what that means. He's probably mad at me for barking *hooray* when the howling stopped. He's going to shoo Nanami and me away.

But wait. What's that? He's carrying a bowl in his hands. And he's smiling.

The two-leg puts the bowl onto the ground. He reaches out his paw.

I don't know if this two-leg is really my friend. Two-legs can be sneaky. A two-leg in London once pretended to

be my friend. He turned out to be a dogcatcher!

Nanami is brave. She goes over and sniffs the two-leg's paw. I think maybe she knows him. She begins to gobble up something from the bowl.

If I don't get over there, she's gonna gobble it all up before I can get any.

I run over to the bowl. *Sniffety, sniff, sniff.* It smells fishy, like salmon kibble. I stick my snout in the bowl and grab a piece with my teeth.

This isn't hard like my kibble. It's squishy.

"This squishy fishy is *yummy, yum, yum*," I tell Nanami.

"It's called sashimi," Nanami explains. "Raw fish."

I take another piece of the squishy
fishy. And another.

While I'm chewing, Nanami
finishes off what's left in the bowl.
She looks up and smiles at the two-
leg who brought the food.

I smile at him, too. Maybe he will
get us more squishy fishy.

But the two-leg doesn't go back
inside. *Boo!* No more squishy fishy
for me.

"Sorry, Sparky," Nanami says. "I have to go to work now. Sayonara."

I don't know for sure what *sayonara* means, but I bet it's good-bye. Because Nanami runs off— leaving me behind.

And then, suddenly, I hear that awful squeaking and squawking again.

Oh no. Not more karaoke! My ears can't take it.

"Wait up!" I call after Nanami. "I'm coming with you."

28

CHAPTER 4

I try to keep up with Nanami. But it's hard. Two-legs on skinny metal machines with only two round paws keep coming between us. They don't move fast. But there are a lot of them. And they don't stop for dogs.

I don't want to stop, either. I don't want to lose Nanami. So I race right past the shops that smell like yummy fish. I swerve around the two-legs on their slow-moving metal machines. And I . . .

Uh-oh.

I don't see Nanami anymore.

I'm all alone. I don't know where I am. I don't know how to get back to Yoyogi Park. How am I going to find my magic bone?

"Hey, you!"

Suddenly, I hear someone. It's not Nanami.

Slowly, I turn around. I see three dogs—two boys and a girl.

"Kon'nichiwa," I say, and I smile proudly. I remembered how they say hello here.

The three dogs do not smile back. They do not say *kon'nichiwa*. They bare their teeth and growl. At *me*.

Did I say it wrong?

I smile wider and try to look friendly. "My name's Sparky. What's yours?"

"Saya," the girl dog growls.

"Takito," the chubby dog says.

"Kaito," the third dog grumbles.

"We're the Ninja Dogs!" they all growl at the same time.

"The *what*-a dogs?" I ask.

The dogs glare and show me their teeth—again.

"Where is she?" Saya demands.

"Where is who?" I reply.

"Don't play dumb," Takito says.

"He's not *playing* dumb," Kaito snarls. "He really *is* dumb if he thinks he can outsmart the Ninja Dogs."

Kaito has something stuck inside his collar. Something bright, beautiful, and sparkly. Something

that smells meaty. Like fried chicken, salmon, and roast beef all rolled into one.

Oh no! Kaito has my magic bone! And by the way it's tucked tightly into his collar, I can tell that *he's holding it prisoner.*

CHAPTER 5

"Where did you get that b-bone?" I ask nervously.

"*We're* asking the questions," Kaito says, stepping closer to me. "What did you do with our queen?"

There's a queen who lives in a big house in London. And there's Queenie, the cat who lives in a yard near me. But I haven't met any queens in Tokyo.

"I don't know your queen," I say.

"You're lying," Saya says.

The dogs puff up their chests and show me their sharp teeth.

I'm trying to not look scared. But a big yellow puddle is forming under me. That happens whenever I'm afraid.

"We demand you return our queen, Nanami," Kaito says.

"Nanami is your *queen*?" I ask.

"Yeah. And we want her back," Kaito says.

My tail tucks itself between my legs. It's scared. And so am I. But Kaito has my bone. So I take a deep breath and try to sound brave.

"I didn't take anyone," I say. "But *you* took my bone. I want it back."

Kaito laughs. "Not so fast, Wizard Dog."

Wizard dog? I've heard of shepherds, terriers, and collies. But never wizards.

"I'm not a wizard dog," I tell him. "I'm a *sheep*dog. And that's my bone."

"It's mine now," Kaito growls.

"You're not getting it back until you tell us where you took our queen."

"How could a little puppy like me take a big dog like Nanami anywhere?" I ask.

"With your magic," Saya answers.

"I don't have any magic," I tell her. "It's the b—"

I stop talking. I don't want the Ninja Dogs to know about the magic in my bone. If they do, they might take a bite of it. Then my bone will be gone forever.

"We saw you do your magic in Yoyogi Park," Takito says. "First you weren't there, and then you were. You just appeared. Like magic."

Now I know how the Ninja Dogs found my bone—they watched me bury it. And then they *un*buried it. There's only one thing I don't understand . . .

"I didn't see you in the park," I say.

"Ninjas are experts at hiding from the enemy," Kaito tells me. "It gives us the element of surprise when we attack."

Element of surprise? Attack? My tail buries itself further between my legs.

"Ninja Dogs are family. Now and forever," Saya declares. "We'll do anything to save Nanami."

"She gave us our jobs," Takito explains. "We owe her."

"What's your job?" I ask him.

"We protect Hachikō," Saya explains.

"What's a *Hachikō*?" I ask.

"Don't you know anything?" Kaito growls.

I step away from him. My whole body starts to shake. This guy is really scary.

"Hachikō was the most faithful Akita ever," Takito tells me. "At the

end of every day, he greeted his two-leg at the train station so they could walk home together."

"Even after his two-leg died, Hachikō kept going to the train station at the end of the day looking for him," Saya continues. "Rain or shine. His loyalty was honored with a bronze statue near the Shibuya train station."

"It's our job to make sure no two-legs climb on the statue, and to see that no dogs pee on it," Kaito adds. "We take turns."

"Nanami never showed up for her turn to guard the statue," Takito says.

"She would never miss her turn. Unless a wizard dog was holding her prisoner in his lair," Kaito growls.

I don't even know what a lair *is*. But I know I want to go home.

"I don't know where Nanami is," I tell Kaito. "Please give me back my bone."

Kaito laughs. "What's so special about the bone, Wizard Dog?"

"The bone could be magic, too," Saya suggests. "I wonder how you turn it on."

"Maybe it has a switch," Takito suggests. "Like a light." He reaches over to Kaito's collar and starts pawing at the bone, looking for a switch.

"Hey, stop," Kaito says. "That tickles."

"Maybe you have to shake the bone to get it to work," Saya suggests.

"Let's try," Kaito agrees. He shakes his body up and down. But that won't make my bone work.

"Please give it back," I plead.

"You'll get your bone when we get Nanami," Kaito says.

"I don't know where she is," I insist. "Only . . ."

The Ninja Dogs crowd around me.

"Only *what*?" Takito demands.

"Only I know where I'd go, if I were Nanami," I say.

The Ninja Dogs glare at me. I gulp, and try not to make another yellow puddle.

"Tell us," Takito insists.

"I'd go find some more of that squishy fishy," I say.

"Squishy fishy?" Kaito asks.

"I think he means sashimi," Saya says. "Maybe he hid her away in the fish market. We should go look."

I don't know what a fish market is, but I'm afraid to ask.

"Give me back my bone, and go

find her," I tell Kaito.

"Oh no," Kaito says. "This bone stays with me until we find our queen. No Nanami, no bone, Wizard Dog. *You're coming with us.*"

CHAPTER 6

"Hurry up, Wizard Dog," Kaito shouts as I trail behind the Ninja Dogs.

The streets of Tokyo are crowded. But I am not going to lose Kaito. No way. I'm keeping my eyes on my bone!

So I keep running. My paws swerve from side to side trying not to bump into two-legs. I keep moving. Fast. Faster. *Fastest.*

Suddenly, I spot something really scary. Even scarier than Kaito. *Giant two-legs!* They're jumping on top of

47

each other and throwing each other to the ground. I stop and stare at them through the window.

The Ninja Dogs stop, too. But they stare at *me*.

"Why is the Wizard Dog stopping at a sumo-wrestling ring?" Takito demands.

Those giants must be called sumos, I think.

"Maybe Nanami *isn't* at the fish market. Maybe she's being held prisoner inside," Saya suggests.

"We'll have to go rescue her," Kaito says.

The Ninja Dogs charge toward the door.

I don't move.

"Let's go, Wizard Dog," Kaito barks to me. "We're going in to see the sumo wrestlers.

"I-I-I'll stay out here," I tell him.

"No, you won't," Kaito says. "You're the one who captured Nanami. And you're the one who's going to set her free."

"But I didn't . . . ," I start to say. Then I stop. Kaito won't believe me, anyway.

I have no choice. If I want my bone, I'm going to have to face the giant sumo wrestlers.

"GRRRRR!"

I hear the sumo-wrestler giants growling the minute I get inside. They're loud. And scary. Just like the Ninja Dogs.

"GRRRR!"

The sumo wrestlers grab each other. They pounce on each other. They throw each other to the ground.

My tail hides between my legs. It's scared. I don't blame my tail. Those shouting, pouncing, throwing, grunting giants are plenty scary.

I don't know why they're so angry. No one has stolen *their* bones.

Wiggle, waggle, wait a minute! The wrestlers just gave me a great idea. I let out a loud, *"GRRRR!"* and

leap on top of Kaito.

Kaito is bigger than I am, but I surprise him. He falls to the ground with me on top of him.

"Get off, Wizard Dog!" he shouts.

"Not until you give me back my bone!" I bark.

"Not until you give us back Nanami!" Kaito growls.

FLIP.

Whoa. Now I'm on my back and

Kaito is on top of me. He's heavy.

"I can't give her back to you," I tell him. My paws are trying to stand up. But Kaito won't let them.

"Then I can't give your bone back," Kaito says.

"Yeah! Kaito's on top!" Takito says. "Beat the Wizard Dog, Kaito!"

"Give me a *K*. Give me an *A*. Give me an *ITO*!" Saya cheers. "Fight, Kaito! Fight!"

"Get off me!" I shout.

Kaito opens his mouth to say something. But before he can, one of the giant sumo wrestlers picks him up and throws him out the door.

"Hey! You can't throw out a Ninja Dog!" Kaito shouts.

I guess the sumo wrestlers don't

speak dog, because they *are* throwing out the Ninja Dogs. A second one has already lifted Takito off the ground and dropped him outside onto the sidewalk.

A minute later, the wrestlers are coming back for Saya. And then me. *Uh-oh.*

There's no way I'm letting those giants near me. I'm getting out of here.

"Go, paws! Go!" I shout. My paws run for the door. I race out onto the sidewalk near Takito and Kaito.

One of the wrestlers carries Saya outside and dumps her onto the ground next to me.

"Hey!" Saya shouts as the sumo wrestlers go back inside. "That hurt!"

"Now what are we supposed to do?" Takito asks Kaito.

Funny. I was thinking the same thing. Wrestling didn't get my bone back from Kaito. Now what am I supposed to do? Before I can *thinkety, think, think* of a new plan, my nose *sniffety, sniff, sniffs* something sweet. It's coming from a pretty little house, just across the street.

Grumble. Rumble. My tummy sure would like something yummy. That squishy fishy didn't fill it for very long.

The sweet smell is all around me. *I just gotta have some!*

"FOOD!" I yelp as I race across the street.

"You can't go in there," Saya

calls after me. "They're having a tea ceremony!"

I don't know what a tea ceremony is. All I know is that nothing is going to keep me from those sweet treats!

CHAPTER 7

"You're not losing us that easily, Wizard Dog," Kaito shouts as the Ninja Dogs race into the little house behind me.

"Where you go, we go," Saya adds. "We will find Nanami."

"Because Ninja Dogs are family, now and forever!" Takito shouts.

I barely hear what they are saying. I'm too busy *sniffety, sniff, sniffing*. Where is that sweet smell coming from?

I spot the treats. Right there.

On the floor. There's a whole plate of them!

My tails starts wagging excitedly. It knows the rule. If food is on the table, it's for two-legs. But any food on the floor is for dogs. And all the sweet treats are on the floor!

The two-legs are sitting on the floor, too. But that doesn't change the rule. *Wiggle, waggle, yum!* Treats, here I come! I take a flying leap toward the treats.

"No, Wizard Dog!" Saya shouts. "The *mochi* is for two-legs!"

"Not if it's on the floor!" I shout back to her. I grab one of the treats in my mouth and swallow it down.

The two-legs leap to their feet. They start shouting.

I hate shouting.

The Ninja Dogs race for the door. They're leaving. Good idea. I gotta get out of here, too.

"Come on, paws!" I bark. "Let's go!"

My paws start running. Fast. Faster. *Fastest!*

My fur flies in my eyes! I can't see anything. I don't know where the door is. But I keep running. Fast. Faster. *Fastest.* Run, run, run.

Crash! I run right through the wall! *Wiggle, waggle, WOW.* I'm

outside now. There's a huge Sparky-shaped hole in the wall where I crashed through. All that wrestling has made me as strong as a sumo wrestler! I can break down walls. I'm a champion sumo puppy!

I shake the fur from my eyes. "Give me back my bone!" I say bravely to the Ninja Dogs, who are all standing beside me on the sidewalk.

"Make me," Kaito replies.

"You should be afraid of me," I tell him. "Didn't you see what I just did? I'm strong. I can crash through walls." I growl and bare my teeth, just to scare them.

The Ninja Dogs look at one another. And then . . . they start laughing.

"Is he kidding?" Takito asks.

Kaito laughs so hard he snorts.

"Why are you laughing?" I growl.

Saya shakes her head. "He's *not* kidding," she says. "I'm wondering if he really is a wizard dog. Wizards should be all-knowing. But this pup doesn't know anything."

Hey! That's not fair. I know lots of stuff. Like I'm not supposed to make yellow puddles in the house. And I'm not supposed to bury my toys in between the couch cushions. And I know that the bone has magic, not me.

But I don't say any of that, because I also know better than to argue with the Ninja Dogs.

"She's right," Takito tells Kaito. "Even a *puppy* wizard would know that the walls of that tearoom are made of rice paper."

Paper? The walls are *paper*?

I glance over at Kaito. He's glaring at me.

The two-legs who were inside the paper room are outside now. They're still yelling. Loudly.

Suddenly I'm not feeling very strong or brave anymore. I'm just sad. No one in Tokyo likes me. Not the two-legs. Not the Ninja Dogs.

"We'd better get out of here," Takito says.

"Yes," Saya agrees. "Those two-legs might call a dogcatcher."

Saya, Takito, and Kaito take off down the street.

Dogcatcher? No way this dog's

getting caught and stuck in a pound in Tokyo. I'm leaving as soon as I can. Which is as soon as I can get my bone back from Kaito.

"Hey!" I shout to the Ninja Dogs. "Wait for me!"

"You're not a wizard, are you?" Saya asks me a little while later when we stop to catch our breath.

I shake my head. "I told you that," I say. "But you didn't believe me."

"There's still something weird about you, Wizard Dog," Takito says.

"My name is Sparky," I tell him.

"Well, there's something weird about you, *Sparky*," Takito corrects himself. "I mean, you did just appear out of nowhere. We all saw you."

"Yeah," Kaito agrees. "And you're a little crazy about this bone."

"That's because it's mine," I tell him. "And I want it back."

"I told you," Kaito says. "When we get Nanami, you get the bone."

I don't want to fight with the Ninja Dogs. I just want my bone back.

"We all want to find Nanami," I tell them. "But we're wasting time arguing with one another. We should work together instead."

The Ninja Dogs stare at me for a minute. My heart starts *thumpety, thump, thumping.*

"He's got a point," Takito says.

"Four brains are better than three," Saya adds.

"Even if one of those brains belongs to a puppy who doesn't know the difference between paper walls and brick walls?" Kaito grumbles.

I don't like Kaito. I don't like giant sumo wrestlers. I don't like shouting two-legs who eat in paper houses.

I want my Josh. I was hoping to be home with him by now. But Kaito has my bone, so I guess I'm going to be later than I thought.

That gives me an idea! "What if Nanami was just late getting to the statue?" I ask the Ninja Dogs. "Maybe she's there now."

"Nanami is never late," Kaito barks.

"Maybe something got in her way that made her late," I say.

"It's possible," Takito agrees.

"There's a first time for everything," Saya says.

"Let's go check the Hachikō statue," I say excitedly.

"We gotta get there fast," Kaito tells us. "You know what that means."

"Sure do," Saya answers.

"Yep," Takito adds.

"Nope," I say nervously.

Kaito gives me a mischievous grin. "Relax. This will be fun."

Relax? With the Ninja Dogs? Is he kidding?

CHAPTER 8

"I can't move!" I try to scream. But the words barely squeak out of me. It's hard to scream when you're squished.

I have followed the Ninja Dogs right into a tiny metal room. There are so many two-legs in this room that the doors could barely close.

But they did, and now there are two-legs to the right of me. Two-legs to the left of me. And Ninja Dogs behind me.

It seems like everything is squishy

in Tokyo. First the fish. Now me.

Suddenly, the floor beneath me starts to move. We're *zoom, zoom, zooming*.

"Aaahhh!" I try to yell. But I'm so smushed that my cries come out softly. "Aaahhh!"

Zoom! Zoom! Zoomee!

"Aaahhh!"

Zoom! Zoom! Zoomee!

Suddenly, the *zooming* stops. The doors open, and the two-legs pour out.

YIKES! I'm being swept away by a sea of trampling two-legs. *Owie!* One of them just stepped on my tail.

"Come on," Takito calls to me as he and the other Ninja Dogs head for the stairs. "We don't have any time to waste."

"Why did we go on that thing?" I ask the Ninja Dogs. "It was horrible."

"The Metro train is the fastest way to get around Tokyo," Kaito explains. "We had to get here fast."

Takito runs toward a statue of an Akita. That must be Hachikō.

"Can you see her? Is Nanami standing guard?" Saya asks Takito.

Takito looks in front. He looks in back. Then he sniffs around.

"Nope," he answers Saya. "And from the smell of it, she hasn't been here all day. Some dog peed here. That wouldn't have happened if Nanami was standing guard."

"Where's Yoshi?" Kaito asks. "He was supposed to be here."

"Is Yoshi another Ninja Dog?" I ask.

"Not even close," Kaito growls angrily.

"Yoshi's a friend of ours," Saya explains. "We asked him to watch the statue while we went looking for Nanami. He must have wandered off."

"Something a true Ninja Dog would *never* do," Kaito grumbles.

Just then, a large mixed-breed dog comes walking over from behind a nearby tree. "Oh, you're back," he says to the Ninja Dogs.

"Where have you been, Yoshi?" Kaito demands. "You were supposed to be guarding the statue while we looked for Nanami."

"I had to go let out some water," Yoshi replies. "If you know what I mean."

We all know what he means.

"Well, while you were letting out water over by that tree, some other dog let out water on Hachikō," Kaito tells him.

"I'm sorry," Yoshi apologizes. "It won't happen again."

"That doesn't matter now," Saya says. "What matters is Nanami. Have you seen her?"

Yoshi shakes his head.

"I told you she wasn't here,

Wizard Dog," Kaito says.

"Sparky," Saya, Takito, and I all correct him.

"Whatever," Kaito replies. He stares at the statue of Hachikō. His tail gets stiff. He grits his teeth.

Kaito sees something, and he doesn't like what he sees. While the Ninja Dogs were busy talking to Yoshi, a two-leg has started to climb on the Hachikō statue.

"Hey, you!" Kaito barks at the two-leg.

"Get down!" Saya shouts angrily.

"Now!" Takito jumps up and bares his teeth.

"What they said," Yoshi adds.

The two-leg looks down. She spots the three Ninja Dogs and Yoshi

jumping up and down. She sees their bared teeth. She hears their barks. And she gets down. Fast. I don't blame the girl. When the Ninja Dogs get angry, they can be plenty scary.

"No one climbs on Hachikō," Takito growls.

"We weren't fast enough," Kaito says. "Nanami would have been on her before she even got one leg on that statue."

"We did okay," Saya assures Kaito. "But we do need Nanami back."

"We never got to the fish market," Takito says. "We could go look for her there."

Saya shakes her head. "We were only going to look for Nanami at the fish market because we thought a wizard dog had taken her there," Saya reminds him. "Sparky's not a wizard. And there's no reason Nanami would have gone to the fish market. No one there ever gives us food."

"True," Kaito agrees. "We need to search places where Nanami might have gone today. And only one of us knows where she was . . ."

The three Ninja Dogs all turn and stare at me.

"Come on, Sparky, think," Saya says. "Where did you and Nanami go after you left the park this morning?"

I *thinkety, think, think* way back to this morning. But it's hard with Kaito glaring at me and scratching himself. Every time he scratches, my bone moves up and down in his collar.

"I just don't get it," Takito groans. "Who would want to hurt Nanami?"

Hurt. *Hurt.* Something hurt me today. What was it? Oh yeah. *My ears!*

"When I was with Nanami, some two-leg hurt my ears really bad," I tell the Ninja Dogs. "She was squeaking and squawking. It was awful."

The Ninja Dogs all look at me strangely.

"What are you talking about?" Takito asks me.

"It was at the place where the two-leg gave us squishy fishy," I tell him.

Kaito rolls his eyes. "Here we go again with the squishy fishy," he says angrily. "How can sashimi hurt your ears?"

"It wasn't the fish," I tell him. "It was the howling. It was awful."

"Howling?" Takito repeats.

"Yes," I insist. "And after the two-leg finished howling, the other two-legs hit their paws together. Their paws made noise. Mine didn't."

I hit my paws together. They still don't make any noise.

"He must mean the karaoke club,"

Saya says. "The one near Yoyogi Park."

"Yes! Yes!" I bark excitedly. "That's what Nanami called it. Karaoke!"

"It's worth checking out," Takito says.

"Let's get moving," Kaito announces. "Yoshi, you stay here. And this time, don't leave the statue alone. Get someone else to stand guard if you need to . . . well . . . you know."

We all know.

"Come on, Sparky," Saya says. "We've got to hurry."

"We're not going back on that Metro thing again, are we?" I ask her nervously.

Saya shakes her head. "Not this time. It'll be faster by paw."

Phew. That's good. Because I don't want to be squishy Sparky ever again.

CHAPTER 9

Squeak! Squawk!

Ow, ow, owie! My ears are hurting.

"See, I told you," I say to the Ninja Dogs as we get closer to the karaoke club. "Two-leg howls really hurt."

"You're not kidding," Takito moans. He covers his ears.

"We have to go in," Saya says. "If Nanami is there, we need to find her. No matter how much it hurts."

"We can take the pain," Kaito

adds. "We're Ninja Dogs."

No. *They're* Ninja Dogs. I'm just a puppy. I don't think I can take the pain.

"You guys go ahead," I say. "I'll wait out here."

Kaito turns and sneers at me. "Remember, I've got the bone."

He's right. I'm going to have to head into the karaoke club. Because where my bone goes, I go.

Squeak. Squawk. Screeeeeech!

Ow! Ow! Owie-ow! The two-leg sounds even worse inside the karaoke club.

"Stop!" My mouth shouts before I can stop it. "Stop howling."

The two-legs inside the karaoke club turn around and stare at me.

Uh-oh. It's never good when two-legs stare like that.

Suddenly, I hear a familiar voice. A dog voice. It doesn't *owie* my ears at all. "Sparky! You came back!"

"Nanami!" I bark. "You're here!"

Nanami pads over. She has a big smile on her face. "I didn't think I'd see you again," she tells me. Then she looks behind me. Her smile gets bigger. "I didn't think I'd see you guys again, either," she tells the Ninja Dogs.

Nanami starts to walk outside. The

Ninja Dogs follow behind her. I follow behind them.

I'm happy that Nanami wants to be outside. The squeaking and squawking is quieter out here.

"It was hard to find you," Saya tells Nanami. "But we didn't give up."

"We're here to rescue you," Takito says.

Nanami gives us a strange look. "Rescue me?" she asks. "From what?"

"From this place," Takito tells her. "From the two-legs holding you prisoner."

"I'm not a prisoner," Nanami tells him. "I'm here because I want to be."

The Ninja Dogs stare at Nanami. Their eyes open wide. Their tails drop. They are definitely surprised.

"That's not true!" Kaito barks.
"You are our queen. You don't belong
with two-legs. You belong with us.

Because Ninja Dogs are family. Now
and forever."

"You don't need me," Nanami tells
him. "You have one another. Masato
had no one, until now."

"Masato?" Takito asks.

"My two-leg," Nanami says. "I've been visiting him for a while now. He always gives me water and food. Today he gave Sparky and me sashimi."

"I remember," I say. "The nice two-leg with the squishy fishy."

"That's him," Nanami tells us. "He owns this karaoke club. We live upstairs."

"This isn't making any sense," Kaito says. "That two-leg isn't alone. Look at all the other two-legs in this club."

"They're his friends," Nanami explains. "And they're nice. But

they come and go. They're not family. Masato was lonely. He needed love. So today, I adopted him."

I know what Nanami means. Sophie is a friend. But she comes and goes. I'm always there for Josh, because Josh and I are family.

But what if Kaito refuses to give me back my bone? What if I can't get home? Josh would be lonely. Will Sophie adopt Josh, just like Nanami adopted her two-leg?

"You're going to stay here with him?" Takito asks.

"Yes," Nanami tells him. "I will be loyal to him, just like Hachikō was loyal to his two-leg. And Masato will be loyal to me. He will feed me, pet me, and love me. And I will protect him and be by his side. That's how it works."

"It actually sounds kind of nice," Takito says.

"It is," I tell him. Because I know.

"It would be wonderful to not have to wander around looking for food," Saya adds.

"It's also great to be petted and scratched," I tell her. "And it's fun to play ball, too."

Takito and Saya both seem to understand why Nanami wants to live with her new two-leg. But Kaito still looks mad.

"I guess that whole thing about us being family, now and forever, wasn't really forever," he barks angrily. "I thought *we* were your family."

And with that, Kaito turns and starts to leave.

"No, Kaito!" I shout. "You can't go."

But Kaito keeps walking away . . . with my bone!

CHAPTER 10

"Kaito! Wait!" Nanami shouts. "Come back here."

Kaito stops. *Phew.*

"Why?" Kaito asks Nanami. "There's nothing else for us to say, is there?"

"Sure there is," Nanami assures Kaito. "We're still a family."

"If you're living in here, and we're living out there, how are we supposed to stay together?" Kaito asks.

Before Nanami can answer, a two-leg walks outside. He's the same two-leg I saw this morning.

When the two-leg spots all us dogs, he stops right in his place. His eyes open wide. Is he scared of the Ninja Dogs, too?

No, he's not. The two-leg is smiling and laughing. He reaches over to pet Saya on the head.

Saya is shy at first. But then she rubs against his leg.

"Masato loves dogs," Nanami says. "Maybe you could all live here with us."

"Really?" Saya asks. "Live with a two-leg indoors?"

Nanami nods.

"Would he feed us, too?" Takito wonders.

"Of course," Nanami replies.

"Maybe he'll give you squishy fishy," I say. "It's delishy."

Nanami looks at Kaito. "What about you?"

"What *about* me?" Kaito asks her gruffly.

"Do you want to stay?" Nanami asks.

"I don't have a choice," he says. "I gotta stay. Ninja Dogs are family.

Now and forever. Except . . ."

"Except what?" Saya asks him.

"Except who is going to guard Hachikō if we aren't there?" Kaito points out.

"Yoshi and his friends could do it," Takito suggests.

"Yeah," Saya agrees. "Yoshi was guarding the statue most of today."

"He did a terrible job," Kaito replies.

"Not so terrible," Takito argues. "And remember, we weren't great when we started, either. He'll grow into being a Ninja Dog."

"Yoshi and his friends can't be the Ninja Dogs," Kaito insists. "*We're* the Ninja Dogs."

"About that . . . ," Nanami begins.

"What?" Kaito barks angrily. "You get us all to say we're gonna live here, and then you tell us we're *not* family?"

"Oh, we're still family," Nanami assures him. "But maybe we should change our name now that we're living here at the karaoke club."

"What about the Karaoke Dogs?" I suggest.

Nanami, Saya, Takito, and Kaito *thinkety, think, think* for a minute.

"I like it," Saya says.

"It has a nice ring," Takito adds.

"The Karaoke Dogs," Nanami repeats slowly. She looks at Kaito. "What do you think?"

Kaito shrugs. "It works."

"Then we're the Karaoke Dogs,"

Nanami says. "And we're family."

"Now and forever," Kaito, Saya, and Takito add.

Good. I'm glad that's settled.

"I want my bone back," I tell Kaito. "We had a deal."

Kaito stares at me. "What's so special about this bone?" he demands. "It's all you've been talking about all day." He turns to the other Ninja . . . I mean, *Karaoke* Dogs.

"You know, we never did find out how Sparky got here. Maybe there's something about this bone . . ."

Kaito scratches at his collar until my bone falls to the ground with a clunk.

"I don't think I'm going to give this bone back after all," he says. "It smells too good. Maybe I'll just take a little bite . . ."

"No!" I bark. Loud. Louder than I've ever barked before. My body begins to shake. My tail tucks between my legs. A puddle starts forming under my feet. He can't bite my bone. He'll *kaboom* away. And I'll be stuck here in Tokyo forever.

"Kaito!" Nanami barks suddenly. "If you made a deal with Sparky, you made a deal. The Ninja Dogs didn't break deals. And neither do the Karaoke Dogs."

Kaito grumbles something under his breath. He sniffs at the bone. He looks at me.

The puddle under my feet is getting bigger.

"Fine," Kaito says finally. He kicks the bone toward me. "Take your silly bone."

He doesn't have to tell me twice. I stop the bone between my paws.

"I'm going home now," I say. I smile at the Karaoke Dogs and Masato. "I'm glad you are still a family."

"Me too," Nanami says.

I look down at my bone. *Sniffety, sniff, sniff.* It smells amazing. Like beef, chicken, and squishy fishy all rolled into one. I open my mouth to take a bite and . . .

"WAIT!" Saya suddenly shouts out.

Oh no! What now?

Saya brings something over to me. It's a piece of paper. Only it's folded to look like a little dog.

"Take this home with you, so you'll always remember us," she says.

I don't think I'll ever forget the Karaoke Dogs. Especially Kaito. He's one scary dog. But I take the gift, anyway.

"Thank you," I tell Saya.

Kaito is eyeing my bone. Any second now, he's just going to leap out and grab it. I can't let that happen.

So I open my mouth wide and *chomp*!

Wiggle, waggle, whew. I feel dizzy—like my insides are spinning all around—but my outsides are standing still. Stars are twinkling in front of my eyes—even though it's daytime! All around me I smell food—fried chicken, salmon, roast beef. But there isn't any food in sight.

Kaboom! Kaboom! Kaboom!

CHAPTER 11

Wiggle, waggle, yippee!

A minute later, I'm back in my yard. There's my tree! And my fence! And my flowers! And the big hole I *duggety, dug, dug* this morning!

I'd better bury my bone again right away. I almost lost it today. I don't want that to happen again.

I place the paper dog Saya gave me on the grass. Then I look around to make sure there are no Ninja Dogs hiding in my yard.

No one is hiding behind the tree.

There's no one on the other side of my fence. I'm alone.

Quickly, I drop my bone into the giant hole. Then I push the dirt back over the bone. It's hidden. No one will find it this time.

Suddenly, I hear something outside the yard. It's Josh's metal machine—the one with four round paws. Josh is home!

Josh! Josh! Josh! My paws race to him. Fast, faster, *fastest*!

My fur falls down in my eyes. I can't see where I'm running. But my paws keep going. Fast. Faster . . .

Boom!

My paws run right into Josh! But he doesn't get angry at me. He just smiles and scratches my ears.

Just then, Josh spots something on the ground near him. He stops scratching and picks up the little paper dog that Saya gave me.

Josh looks at the paper dog. Then he looks at me, his real dog.

I wish I could tell Josh that the paper dog is a gift from a friend in Tokyo. I wish I could tell him about the squishy fishy, and the sumo wrestlers, and Hachikō, and the Ninja Dogs who are now the Karaoke Dogs.

But I don't speak two-leg. And Josh doesn't speak dog. So I roll over onto my back and smile.

Josh laughs. He bends down, and starts scratching my belly. *Scratchity, scratch, scratch!* Josh is the best scratcher in the world.

Sometimes dogs and two-legs don't need words. There are lots of ways to say I love you. And if you ask me, *scratchity, scratch, scratching* is one of the best.

I'm happy to be back with Josh. This is where I belong. Because he and I are family. *Now and forever.*

Fun Facts about Sparky's Adventures in Tokyo

Yoyogi Park

Yoyogi Park is one of the largest parks in Tokyo. It has lawns, ponds, and forests. Back in 1964, it was the site of the Olympic village where athletes from all over the world gathered for the Olympic Games. Today, Japanese teens like to gather at Yoyogi park to sing, dance, and hang out with friends.

Karaoke

Karaoke comes from the Japanese words *kara*, which means "empty," and *oke*, short for *ōkesutora*, which means "orchestra." Tokyo has many karaoke clubs where people gather to sing their favorite songs onstage while using recorded background music. Singing in a karaoke club lets people pretend to be just like their favorite performers.

Sumo Wrestlers

Japanese sumo wrestlers have been competing against one another for more than one thousand years. That makes sumo wrestling Japan's oldest sport. Today's sumo wrestlers dress a lot like wrestlers did centuries ago, with their hair in a knot at the top of their heads and a simple cloth tied around their waists. Sumo matches take place in a wrestling ring called a *dohyō*. During a match, the wrestlers try to throw or tackle each other. The one who forces his opponent out of the ring or down onto the mat is the winner.

Japanese Tea Ceremony

Japanese people have been serving tea and treats to honored guests for hundreds of years. During a tea ceremony, bitter green tea and sweet rice cakes called *mochi* are served. Not just anyone can serve tea and treats at a Japanese tea ceremony. People go to school to learn how to make and serve the tea correctly.

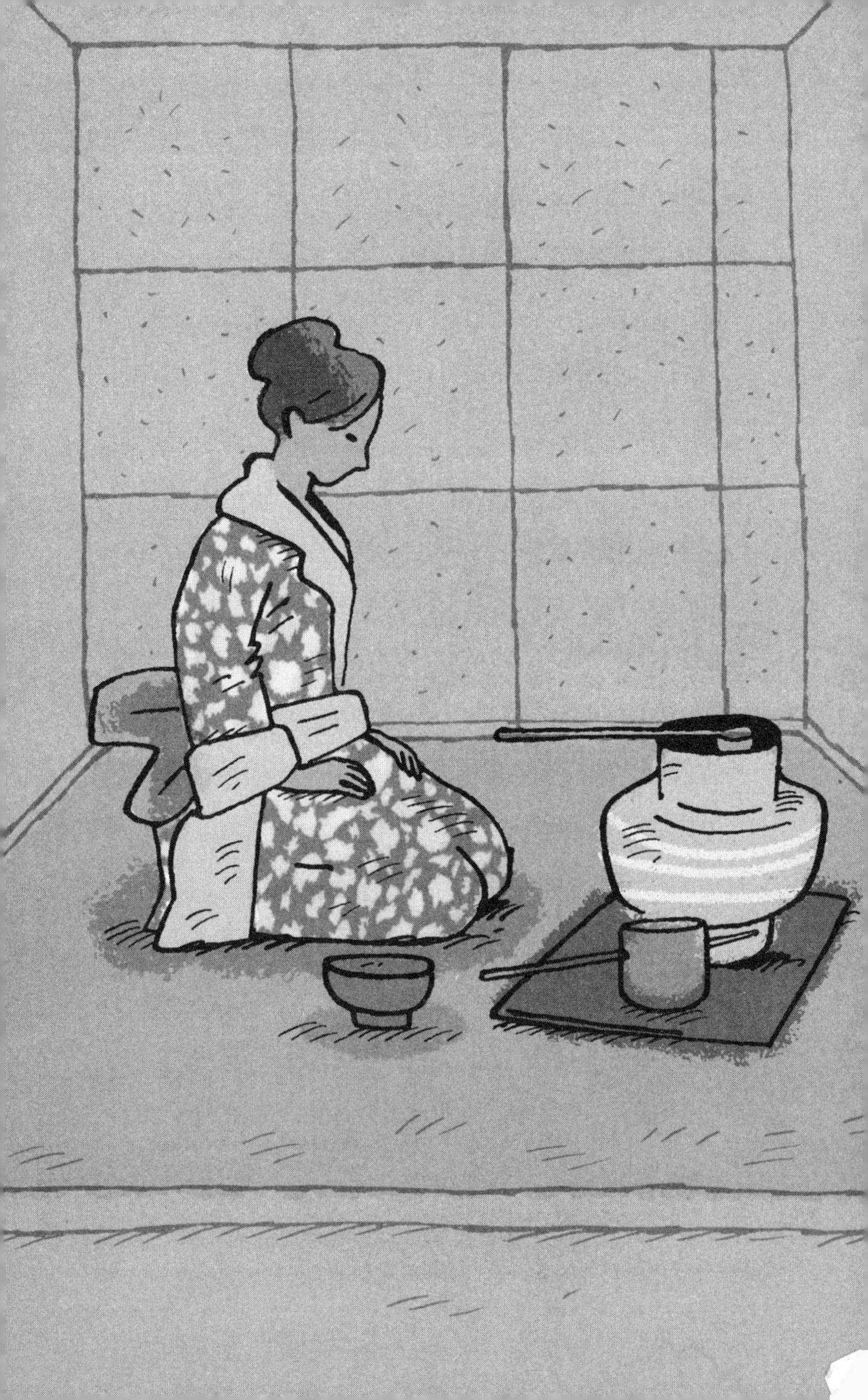

Origami

The traditional Japanese art of paper folding began centuries ago. Origami sculptures are made by folding a flat sheet of paper into a design. Cutting and gluing are not allowed. While origami can be done with any sheet of paper, the traditional paper, called *washi*, is made from bark from the gampi tree or the mulberry bush. It also can be made from hemp, rice, or wheat.

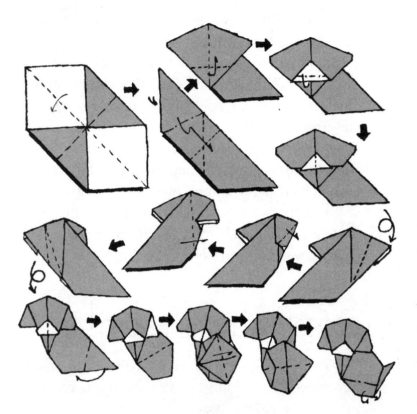

About the Author

Nancy Krulik is the author of more than 200 books for children and young adults, including three *New York Times* Best Sellers. She is best known for being the author and creator of several successful book series for children, including Katie Kazoo, Switcheroo; How I Survived Middle School; and George Brown, Class Clown. Nancy lives in Manhattan with her husband, composer Daniel Burwasser, and her crazy beagle mix, Josie, who manages to drag her along on many exciting adventures without ever leaving Central Park.

About the Illustrator

You could fill a whole attic with Seb's drawings! His collection includes some very early pieces made when he was four—there is even a series of drawings he did at the movies in the dark! When he isn't doodling, he likes to make toys and sculptures, as well as bows and arrows for his two boys, Oscar and Leo, and their numerous friends. Seb is French and lives in England. His website is www.sebastienbraun.com.

31901059468316